Don't Call Me Chicken

Titles in the Harvestime **Pressure Points** series:

Other books by Peggy Burns:

Don't Call Me Chicken

Peggy Burns

Illustrations: Liz Priestley

Harvestime

Published in the United Kingdom by:
Harvestime Services Ltd, 12a North Parade, Bradford
West Yorkshire BD1 3HT

ISBN 0 947714 20 0

Typeset by in the United Kingdom by:
Grassroots Limited, London N3 2LJ

Printed and bound in the United Kingdom by:
Richard Clay Ltd., Bungay, Suffolk

Contents

1

Zac

There's been an empty seat next to me in school ever since Ian Mincher went to live in Birmingham. So when this new kid joined our class he was bound to end up sitting next to me.

He said his name was Donald Cusack and dared me to call him anything but Zac. He seemed like a good sort, so I didn't.

I soon found out that that kid wasn't like anybody I'd ever known. The first thing he did was to take a big hairy spider out of a matchbox he had in his pocket and put it on Kelly Paget's arm. She didn't notice it at first, not until it started walking. Then she let out this almighty screech, flung her English book in the air and went completely bananas.

Of course, the guys thought it was great — they all fell about laughing, while the girls squealed and pranced around, searching for the spider. All except

Sophie Batchelor, that is. Sophie Batchelor wouldn't bat an eye at a king-size tarantula.

It was about ten minutes before Mr Newton could make himself heard. He banged on the desk, then looked at me over the top of his glasses.

'Matt Graham,' he said, when the racket had died down a bit. 'Do I have you to thank for this interruption?' He had to blame me, of course. I suppose he couldn't believe that any new kid could start acting the fool when he'd only been in the school a couple of hours.

I said, 'No, Sir.'

He fixed me with a stare that would have daunted a firing squad. 'That spider materialised in your vicinity,' he said. (He always talks like that.) 'Where did it come from?'

'A mummy spider,' shouted some joker from the back of the room.

'My, my — we have a humorist in our midst. Johnson? I thought so. You really must consider a career in show business.' Mr Newton shoved the glasses back up his nose with the tip of his finger. 'The next comedian can count on having 500 lines.'

Nobody risked it.

By the end of that first day, Zac had turned biology test papers into paper darts, nicknamed Mr Pye, the maths teacher, 'Sweetie' (it made a change

from 'R-Squared', which is what he's usually
called), drawn a cartoon of Mr Newton on the
blackboard, with a nose as red as Rudolph's and
with his glasses halfway down it, and put a whoopee
cushion on Mrs Gray's chair. (This last trick didn't
work because she saw it before she sat down, and
confiscated it.)

He'd made enemies of all the staff except Mr
Harnett, the games teacher — not bad going for
a first day in school.

I found out something else about Zac. He plays
the best game of football of anybody in the school,
and that's saying something. I could see that old
Harnett already had him marked out for centre
forward in the school team.

We walked home together after school, and it
turned out that Zac's family live in the old haunted
house in Warwick Street — they moved in last
week.

Not that anybody really believes in all that stuff
about the place being haunted. It's just that it's
been empty for about two years and the paint is
peeling off the doors and the garden looks like a
jungle. But Robbo King says he once saw a blue
light moving from room to room. And some others
had seen a flash of something white at a bedroom
window. The little kids from the junior school dare

each other to sneak into the garden and peep through the windows.

Nobody ever expected the place to be lived in again, but Zac said they bought it because it was going cheap.

The house still looks a bit of a mess but Zac said they're going to start doing it up soon and make it really fantastic. At least there are some nice flowered curtains in the windows now. Before, they looked horrible, like empty, staring eye sockets.

Some of the guys told Zac about the ghosts but he didn't seem very impressed.

He invited me in, but I knew my mum would have tea ready, so I thought I'd better not.

After that, I saw a lot of Zac. As well as sitting together at school, we started going up to the park in the evenings and on Saturday mornings to kick a ball around. He plays a really ace game — you should see the way he controls the ball. I learned a lot from him about playing football.

I told Zac I'd get my mother to invite him for tea. He said he had a whole boxful of football programmes, and he'd bring it with him when he came.

I hit a snag, though, when I asked my mother if he could come round. She looked down her nose and sniffed. She didn't need to say anything. I could tell she didn't want him to come.

I said, 'What have you got against him? Zac's OK when you get to know him.'

She swished soapsuds around in the kitchen sink and dropped my school shirts into the water.

Don't you see enough of him in school?' she said, rubbing at the collar of one of the shirts. 'Why don't you ask Andy? You get on well with Andy — he's supposed to be your best friend. And he's a nice boy.'

'So is Zac. Andy came last week — you know he did.'

Andy's my mate from our church. I like him, and he comes here a lot. But I wanted Zac for a change.

'What's wrong with Zac?' I said again. 'Why don't you want him to come?'

She stopped rubbing at the shirt. 'I don't know, really...it's just that I heard some things about him that I didn't like. I wouldn't want you to get too friendly with him, Matt.'

'Mum — you've never even *met* him. How can you tell what he's really like? Zac's OK. Honest.'

She sighed again. 'Oh, I guess you're right. I suppose I'm not being fair to the boy, judging him by what people say about him.'

I bet I knew some of the things they said, too.

'Sweetie' Pye lives near us, up on the Colston road. And he'd been one of the first to declare war on Zac. He always calls him Donald, and that makes Zac madder than anything else.

In the end, though, I managed to talk my mother round, and Zac came home with me after school on Friday.

What a pity I didn't listen to her. Things would have been a whole lot easier for me!

2

A prize wally

The first thing I did when we got in was to get the tablecloth out of the cupboard and spread it over the table. Normally I don't think anything about doing things like that — laying the table's my regular job. But Zac stared at me like I was in a zoo or something.

I said, 'What's up?'

Zac looked at me and rolled up his eyes to the ceiling. He's always doing things like that. As if he knows everything, and everybody else is a pack of idiots. That's one thing about him that I don't like much.

'I'd like to see anybody try to make *me* set the table, that's all,' he said.

I couldn't tell him that I did it all the time. Suddenly feeling like a prize wally, I opened a drawer and fished out some table mats, then dumped some knives and forks on the table. The job wasn't done right, but I could feel Zac's eyes boring holes in my back.

Sophie Batchelor is the only other person who can make me feel like that. She lives just a few doors away. She came round yesterday to borrow a square cake tin for her mother (What did she want to bake a square cake for?) and, of course, I happened to be washing dishes.

She stood there in the kitchen doorway, grinning like a Cheshire cat, watching me. She just loved it. It would have to be her.

Sophie Batchelor says she's a feminist — she believes in women's lib and all that. She says that girls are every bit as good as boys. (I think they probably are, but I'd eat worms rather than tell *her* that!)

She says that when she grows up she's going to be a mechanic and when she gets married she'll go out to work at the garage while her husband stays at home to look after the babies. I'm glad I won't be the one who's married to her.

Zac said, 'Do you have to do this sort of stuff all the time? You poor guy! Catch *me* letting women boss me around like that — you want to tell them straight. What about Beth? Let her do it.'

I shrugged my shoulders. 'She's taking exams,'

I told him. 'She has a lot of studying to do.'

Beth is my sister. Her name isn't Elizabeth — which is what most people think — it's Bethan. We all call her Beth. She's nearly 16 and thinks she's the greatest. She's in her exam year at school so she doesn't have to do so much work around the house. I notice she always has time to do her hair every day though, and talk to Simon Cook on the phone.

I kept that bit to myself. I didn't want Zac's pity. After all, jobs are jobs. I'd never thought it mattered all that much who did them. Even Dad has been known to pick up a tea-towel.

'It's stupid, having to do women's work,' Zac went on, laying it on thick. 'I don't have to do it. Neither does Robbo. Tell *her* that.'

'It wouldn't do any good. She says that some day I might be a student and live in digs, and what would I do then if I didn't know how to look after myself?'

My mum's no feminist, though. According to her, God made men and women as good as each other, only different. That figures, when you come to think about it. I mean, they're *built* different, for a start. I couldn't see my mum lugging sacks of cement around, for instance. Or my dad baking a batch of fairy cakes, either. And if God had wanted to, he could have made everybody the same.

It's different for Zac. His family's not a bit like mine. My dad always tells us we should all pitch in and help each other. At Zac's place it seems like it's everyone for himself. I don't think I'd like that much, though Zac's lucky in some ways. He gets to do whatever he wants. He even stays out till ten or eleven o'clock.

His mother doesn't seem to mind what he does or where he goes, as long as he keeps out of her hair. Like today, when I'd asked him to tea. He'd said OK, but I don't think he told his mum he wouldn't be home. I'm glad my mum's not like that.

Zac had forgotten to bring the football programmes after all, and it was raining outside, so there wasn't much to do. We went into the lounge and sat down on the sofa.

Our cat Snowball jumped up straightaway — she loves sitting on people's knees. I'm not supposed to let her, though, since my mother found out last week she has fleas.

I could have told her that if she'd asked me. They come on my bare arms sometimes and feel tickly-prickly. But I don't care. Beth says I'm disgusting and she won't go near the cat now. Mum sprayed her with some stuff (the cat, not Beth) and she's going to buy a flea collar next time she's in town.

I said, 'What shall we do? I could bring my computer down if you like.'

'What games have you got?'

'I haven't got many, yet. I only got the computer at Christmas so I'm still getting games together.'

'Have you got *Demon Warrior?*'

I shook my head.

'You haven't got *Demon Warrior!*' He looked at me pityingly. 'What about *Revenge of the Undead?*'

I shook my head again.

'Let's not bother, then. Let's see what's on telly instead.'

He got up and switched on the TV set. Nobody said he could.

At this time of day the programmes are mostly cartoons and kid's stuff. But today there was a film on that looked like it might be good. It had this weird spooky music. I could see it was going to be the sort of film my mum and dad don't like me watching — they're fussy about what books I read, too. (My dad always says, 'If you want your mind to be a dustbin, fill it with rubbish.')

So they make me turn off this kind of stuff. When the kids at school are talking about TV programmes it usually turns out that I've missed them. I couldn't tell Zac that, though. He'd die laughing.

He watches whatever he wants to — even when it finishes late. Nobody switches the set off and tells *him* to go to bed.

I think my dad takes things a bit far, to be honest. After all, what harm could seeing a film possibly do? I mean, it's not as if it was *real,* only actors playing parts. Everybody knows that. I reckon my dad's too particular.

Zac unwrapped a Yorkie bar, broke it and passed half to me. That's another thing — he gets a lot more sweets than I do.

'It's nearly teatime,' I told him. 'My mum's making lasagne, and she won't half be mad if we can't eat it all.'

'I've got a good appetite.' He tossed a piece of chocolate into the air, caught it in his mouth and started to chew. He nodded towards the TV set. 'You want thish on?' he said, rather slushily.

I nodded, my mouth full. 'Might as well.'

My mum was cooking. Dad was working overtime. They weren't going to know what we were watching, were they? 'What the eye doesn't see . . . .'

The film was great. It was about this girl called Becky who went into this house where there was a scruffy old man asleep on a bed with all his clothes on. I don't know why she went there — we'd missed that part. Then the music started going thump...thump...thump, like somebody's heart beating, and you knew something nasty was going to happen.

It got louder and louder and faster and faster as the girl walked towards this big cupboard. You saw a close-up of her eyes as she opened the door, and she looked like she was scared stiff. You were sure there was going to be a skeleton inside it, or a dead body, or something like that. But there wasn't. It was just an old box on a shelf.

There was something scary inside the box though — you could tell — and I didn't want to look when she opened it, but I had to. My own heart was thumping nearly as fast as the music!

The girl lifted the lid — and this horrible red light poured out of it and filled the whole place, as if it was on fire, and the girl screamed like she was being murdered.

Then the light died away and there was this strange look in her eyes, like she'd gone crazy or something. It turned out she wasn't herself any more; she was possessed by the spirit of this witch who'd been burnt at the stake in sixteen-something.

The girl turned the old man into a raving lunatic just by looking at him, and then started making chairs and tables and plates throw themselves around without even touching them. In the end they took her away to the Funny Farm.

I thought it was an ace film. But Zac said if I wanted to go round to his house tomorrow, he'd show me something better. I wanted to know what it was, but he wouldn't tell me any more than that.

The guy on TV said there was going to be another film in the same series at the same time next week — *Witch-finder's Sabbath*. It sounded good, so we decided that Zac would come home with me again so we could watch it together.

3

Frank's video

I found out the next morning what Mrs Batchelor had wanted the cake tin for. When I got back from playing football with Zac there was an envelope stuck in the letterbox. It was addressed to me — in Sophie's squashy handwriting. I'd know it anywhere. What was Sophie Batchelor writing to me for?

I tore it open.

It was an invitation to her birthday party the following Sunday. She'd written on the bottom, *'Please bring a record'*, and underlined it. That meant they were going to be dancing. I groaned.

My mother said, 'What is it?' and I passed her the card.

'An invitation — how nice!'

'Do I *have* to go?'

'I thought you liked parties.'

'It depends on the party. They're going to have dancing. And it's a *girl's* party. What do I want to go to *Sophie Batchelor's* party for? I can't *stand* her.'

'There'll be plenty to eat.'

Now there she had something. And if I knew Mrs Batchelor it wouldn't be rotten old egg sandwiches and jelly. More like hot dogs with barbecue sauce, and pizzas, and burgers.

I said, 'If I do go, I'm not doing any dancing. And I'm not going to play any soppy games like pass the parcel and postman's knock either.'

'Hmph. I should think Sophie's more likely to arrange five-a-side football.'

My mother has Sophie Batchelor figured out.

'What can we do about a present?' she went on. 'It's going to be difficult to hit on the right thing.'

I knew what she meant. You don't get bracelets and earrings and stuff for a girl like Sophie.

'They've got piranha fish round at the pet shop,' I said. 'Get some of those. Or how about a box of stink-bombs?'

But in the end we bought a pencil-case shaped like a telephone box, and a set of felt pens to go inside it. Very boring. Not a patch on piranha fish.

Later on I asked my mum if I could go to Zac's for tea. She said yes, but I don't think she really wanted me to go. She hadn't changed her mind about him in spite of his coming here the day before.

Maybe she'd have liked him a bit more if he'd had better manners and got his hair cut. He's got blue eyes and fair hair, like me, only his hair is about a mile long. My mother moans if mine grows to my ears.

Although Zac's name is Donald Cusack, his mother is Mrs Webb. I thought that was funny till he told me his mum and dad got a divorce a few years ago and she married somebody else. Zac's stepfather is a lorry driver called Frank Webb, and Zac calls him Old Spider (Spider — Webb. Get it?). Not to his face, of course. He wouldn't dare. He says Frank's got a foul temper.

When I got there, Zac's mum was drying nappies in front of the fire. Zac's got a baby sister. Well, half-sister, I suppose. I wish I had one instead of bossy Beth. If she was younger than me, *I* could do the bossing.

Mrs Webb was surprised to see me — the wally hadn't even told her I was coming. I wished he had. But she was nice to me and cooked egg and chips and apple crumble. It was just as good as anything *my* mum makes.

'Can I have some money?' Zac asked his mother after tea.

'You're always wanting money for something,' she said. 'I gave you a pound yesterday, and you had your spending money at the weekend. Money goes through your fingers like water.'

'Aw, come on, Mum. Don't be mean. We want some chocolate.'

'You eat too much chocolate. You won't have a tooth left in your head by the time you're 20 — every penny I give you, you spend on sweets. You're not getting anything more out of me this week so you needn't bother asking.'

'Aw Mum!'

She didn't even look up.

She lifted the baby into a high-chair and started spooning stuff from a jar into its mouth. It ran out down the baby's chin and Mrs Webb scraped it off and shoved it back in again. It took about four goes to get rid of one spoonful. I figured a meal would take all night at that rate.

'Where's your dad?' I asked Zac.

'You mean Frank. He's not my dad.'

'Don't be so touchy. You know who I mean.'

'He's gone to Glasgow today. He won't be home. He'll go straight to the pub when he gets back.'

'What was it you wanted to show me?'

'Ssh.' He tipped his head in his mum's direction. 'You'll see. She'll be going out soon. She won't miss her Saturday night bingo. I'll show you when she's gone. Come on, let's go round to the shop.'

'What with? *I* haven't got any money.'

'No sweat.'

We went out into the hall. Mrs Webb's shoulder-bag hung on a hook among a lot of coats. Zac unzipped it and felt about inside. 'Rats,' he said. 'She's gone and hidden it again.'

'What are you looking for?'

He opened a drawer in the hall stand, and then the other. Then he felt in some of the coat pockets. 'Got it.'

'What?'

'This.' He pulled out a brown purse and opened it.

'Zac — no! Don't do that! She said you couldn't . . . .'

'You really *are* a kid, aren't you?'

He was the same age as me but he made me feel about six years old.

'This is what she *expects* me to do. She hides it in different places all the time, but I always find it. It's like a game we play. Every now and again she goes crazy and wallops me, but she couldn't hurt a fly. It's Frank you've got to watch. Now if she told *him* . . . .'

He left the sentence unfinished. It spoke for itself.

He took a pound coin out and shoved the purse back into the coat pocket. 'Come on.'

We went around to the Corner Cabin — that's the local sweet shop. It's called that because it's a wooden kiosk sort of place, on the corner of School Street.

Zac bought a couple of Mars bars, and we sat on Jackson's garden wall to eat them. But that chocolate didn't taste right somehow.

Later on that evening Mrs Webb went out to bingo, just like Zac had said she would. She told him she'd already put the baby to bed, but he was to keep an eye on her. He pulled a face at that.

'Some people don't make their kids work for nothing,' he said. 'Stingy old witch. I reckon you ought to pay me so much an hour for babysitting.'

I thought she'd hit him — my mother would have done if I'd said that to her. She says she can't stand cheeky kids. But Mrs Webb went out without saying anything.

As soon as she'd shut the door behind her, Zac stood on a chair and took a video tape off the top of the kitchen cupboard.

'Frank belongs to a private video club. He gets these all the time. He thinks I don't know, but I found out months ago. He always hides them up there. He'd kill me if he knew I watched them!'

'What is it?' I asked him.

'A film.'

'Well I didn't think it was a book of fairy stories. What's it about?'

'Wouldn't you like to know?'

Zac can make you hopping mad without trying too hard. I said, 'Is it something like the film we saw on TV yesterday?'

'That? That was nothing. I'm telling you — you've never seen anything like *this* before.'

He slotted the film into the video, grinning round at me.

And at that moment I knew it was all wrong for me to be here. I don't know what made me feel that way — maybe it was the way he grinned like that.

I wished I hadn't come. But how could I go home now, before the film had even started? Besides, part of me really wanted to see what it was like. It's a funny sort of feeling, wanting something and not wanting it both at the same time.

Perhaps I could watch for a few minutes and then say I had to go home. I'd stay for the first half hour. Just to see what it was about. . . .

The film was called *Ghouls from the Pit of Hell,* and it was horrible.

It was the horriblest, awfulest thing I'd ever seen.

I'm not even going to write down what it was about because I never knew they were allowed to film stuff like that. It was sick!

I sat and watched it for a while. It was so scary I felt hot and sweaty all over, and my heart was pounding so fast I thought Zac would be able to hear it.

I tried reminding myself that the blood was only red paint and the whole thing was just a story being acted out, but it didn't work because it *seemed* so real. I sat back in my chair and tried taking deep breaths.

'It's great, isn't it?' said Zac. 'You just watch what comes next. This is a good bit. Wait till you see the close-ups. . . . The guy gets locked into this room — he can't get out, see? And then the walls start closing in on him, real slow, and he's screaming, and there's all these spikes sticking out of the walls. . . .'

He didn't have to say what came next. I had a pretty good idea, and I didn't want to see the close-ups. I shut my eyes.

Zac saw me, of course.

'What's up? You're not chicken, are you?' he said. He flapped his elbows, clucking like a hen, and then laughed.

I grinned back, a bit weakly. 'Course not.' If

there's one thing I can't stand, it's being laughed at.

So I stuck it out. My stomach felt exactly like I'd eaten too much ice-cream, but I watched it all the way through, and then I went home.

I only lived a few streets away, but I walked slower and slower — like an old man. My legs and my feet felt like lead. There was something weighing me down. I was heavy all over, and I felt sick. Not in my stomach, but inside somewhere. If I'd known the film was going to be as bad as that I wouldn't have gone round there in the first place.

I'd always thought that there couldn't possibly be anything wrong with watching a film, and that my dad was carrying things a bit too far. But that was before. Now I've changed my mind.

Maybe my dad knows what he's talking about after all.

4

The dream is real

I was dreaming.

In the dream, I was sitting on the couch in front of the TV, watching a film. Sophie Batchelor had somehow got into it (What was I doing, dreaming about *her*?), and I was watching her creep around this dark, spooky old house. She was going into one dusty, spidery room after another, looking for something. I didn't know what.

And then I saw that in one of the rooms a man was hiding behind the door, waiting for her to step inside. He had a long, thin knife in his hand — the sharp kind that butchers use.

It was dark but you could see the moon through the window and there was a shaft of light across the middle of the room. Every time the man moved, the moonlight glittered on this horrible knife.

Then Sophie pushed the door and it opened

slowly, its hinges creaking softly. I was trying to shout out to warn her but I couldn't speak. The words stuck in my throat — there wasn't a thing I could do!

She took a step into the room.

There was a stealthy movement behind the door, then the glint of steel. I heard a choking scream. The next minute she was lying on the floor with blood spreading out in a great pool all around her.

Sophie was moaning and sobbing. I knew she was dying and I had to get help — somehow the film had become real and I was there in the house with her. I turned to run out — but right behind me was the guy with the knife. And he was coming for *me*.

I let out a shout — and found I was sitting up in bed, shaking from head to foot, my heart thumping like a jungle drum. I was shivering with cold — yet I was wet through with perspiration. I wondered if I'd really cried out or if it had only been in my dream.

I lay down again, staring up into the darkness, my heart pounding. I could still hear Sophie's moaning, but now that I was awake, I knew it was the wind, wailing in the chimney.

Listening carefully, I could hear another noise, too. It had been part of my dream — but I knew it was here, now. Somewhere out on the landing, outside my bedroom door. A kind of strangled gurgling noise, followed by a quick 'plip'. It stopped, then started again. Gurgle, burble...plip. It was horrible.

I felt myself go rigid all over, and my skin prickled with sweat. What could it be? A cut throat...the death rattle...blood dripping? I tried to swallow and couldn't.

The very worst thing was, I had to go to the loo. I *had* to go...And what would I see, out there on the landing?

I reached over to snap on my bedside lamp, and remembered. Beth borrowed it to do homework in her room. The switch broke on hers.

I took a deep breath and sat up again. I had to walk from the bed to the door *in the dark*.

What if there was someone hiding under my bed? Someone with a long, shiny knife, razor-sharp, waiting there for me. Just waiting for me to put a foot out....

I wanted to call for my dad, but how could I? A kid of my age!

'God — please help me,' I prayed. 'I'm scared! Don't let me be afraid anymore.'

We always pray about everything in our house. God *does* answer when you ask him for help. I know,

because I talk to him all the time, ever since I asked
Jesus into my life at camp last summer.

But, tonight, praying wasn't making any
difference to the way I felt, and I didn't know why.
I was just as scared as ever.

I hated that noise the wind was making, moaning
and sighing around the house. Ours is the last house
in an old terrace, right at the top of a steep hill
where we catch every breath of wind.

On bonfire night you can see fires dotted about
all over the city from my bedroom window. You
get a free firework display, too — rockets going up
all over the place. I like living here — apart from
that awful noise the wind makes on nights like this.

Ivy stems were brushing against the glass,
tapping like bony fingers. My curtains were moving
around, billowing out as if there was someone
hiding inside them. Commonsense told me that it
was only the draught from the open window, but
it looked exactly like someone waiting there, by the
window, ready to leap out.

I stared as hard as I could into the darkness. Was
that black lump under the window-sill a pair of
shoes, half-hidden under the curtains? *Were there feet
inside them?*

It wouldn't be easy to get in at my bedroom
window. But with a ladder, someone could do it.

I had my plans all ready for the day I heard a burglar climbing in. I was going to run out of the bedroom door and lock it behind me — there was a bolt on the outside at the top — then I'd nip out of the back door and pinch the burglar's ladder. After that I'd ring the police and they'd come and collect the burglar and give me a medal — and maybe a reward.

Only now, when there really *might* be somebody hiding there, I didn't feel much like running outside to heave ladders around in the dark.

Why wasn't I brave and strong and afraid of nothing? At school, I'd acted tough, along with all the other kids. That's easy when you're with five or six other guys and there's no real danger. But have you noticed how hard it is to be tough, once you're on your own?

I licked my lips. My whole mouth was dry. I had to go to the bathroom. How was I going to get there?

There was only one thing to do — and I was ashamed of myself for thinking of it. I'd have to jump from the bed, as far as I could in one go, switch on the big light, then hare across the landing to the bathroom before anything could get me.

I stood up on the bed and took a flying leap — and landed with a foot right on the edge of the board

that held my electric train track. I felt like I was
crippled for life. The board tipped and sent all the
engines and carriages thundering across the floor
like an earthquake.

I switched on the light quickly, and hopped and
limped as fast as I could along the landing — there
was nothing scary there that I could see — and into
the bathroom.

When I came out my dad was standing there in
his pyjamas, rubbing his eyes. Was I glad to see
him!

'Are you all right?' he said. 'What happened?'

'A few broken bones, that's all. I fell over my
train set.'

'You fell over a *train set?* I thought we'd been hit
by a DC10!'

My dad can be very corny at times.

'How's the broken foot?' he said.

'I might have to use crutches for a few weeks,
but I'll survive.'

I had a quick look under my bed. There wasn't
much there. Just the usual stuff, my old Star Wars
spaceship and a Transformer robot that I don't play
with any more, a Bible, a few toffee papers and a
couple of odd rolled-up socks that needed washing.

I jumped back into bed. Dad shut the window
and clicked off the light.

'Goodnight, Dad.'

'Goodnight, sleep tight, mind the bugs don't bite,' he quoted.

I didn't sleep tight, though. I'd forgotten to ask about the noise on the landing — and it was still there.

I lay awake for a very long time.

5

The noise

I jumped, and opened my eyes. I'd been so sure I'd never sleep but in the end, of course, I had. Now the sun was pouring in through a gap in the curtains. The long night, with its horrible dreams, was over, but it had left me with a thumping headache. It was the worst headache I'd ever had, right behind my eyes.

The sunshine made it worse, so I closed my eyes again — and that rotten video we'd watched floated back into my mind as if we'd only just switched off the TV set. My heart started banging away in my chest just *thinking* about it.

Would I ever forget it? I tried to imagine what it would be like to feel like this for the rest of my life.

Zac watches this sort of junk all the time. I wondered how he'd felt when he first started. Had he felt like me — or was I just being a coward? He'd fall about laughing if he knew how scared I'd been.

Perhaps watching those films is something you get used to — the more you watch, the less it bothers you! Zac *enjoys* them now. How can he?

I thought, 'What kind of a mind do you have to have, to actually *like* that stuff? *What kind of a mind does Zac have?*'

I turned over in bed and pulled the duvet over my head. I didn't want to think about Zac like that. Zac was my friend, and he was OK.

I'm glad he'd never know how scared I'd been in the middle of the night. That crazy noise! I wondered what had made it. Was it still there? I pushed the quilt back and sat up in bed, listening.

Five houses away, Sophie Batchelor's poodle was howling. It howls like that all the time. Their next-door neighbour keeps saying he'll take them to court about the dog being a nuisance, but he never does.

As well as that, I could hear the milk-float going down Mansfield Terrace with all the crates and bottles rattling. A couple of pigeons croodled outside my window.

In the quietness of the night the noise had sounded quite loud. Now you could hardly hear it — but underneath all the other sounds, it was still there. A quiet guggle-glug. . .guggle-glug. . .plip.

It was different in the daylight. I still didn't like it much, but it wasn't so scary. I got out of bed and went to investigate. I stuck my head round the bedroom door.

A sticky crimson pool was oozing slowly from under the airing cupboard door and across the vinyl floor.

It was just like my nightmare. I remembered how Sophie had looked, clutching the knife-wound in her side, the blood soaking her clothes and spreading across the dirty floorboards.

I felt my knees go weak. That had been a bad dream — but this was *real*. I stood clutching the doorpost, watching that slow red stream. Listening to that soft, horrible bubbling sound.

I swallowed. Whatever this was, I had to make myself do something about it. I forced my unwilling legs to carry me across the landing. I got ready to run, then flipped open the door, just like the cops do on TV.

What I saw wasn't a corpse, dripping blood. It was a demijohn that my dad uses to make wine, with dark red frothy liquid rising up inside the glass jar, and the airlock on top bubbling away like crazy. Even the water in the airlock had turned pink, and wine was leaking out of it, down the sides and all over the cupboard floor.

Blackberry wine, made with last autumn's blackberries from the freezer. I remembered, now, hearing Dad say he was going to make it.

I shut the door, grinning with relief. Beth came out of her bedroom tying up her dressing-gown. How did she do it? She'd just got out of bed but she didn't have a hair out of place. I knew without looking that I was like a scarecrow.

'Hi, baby brother,' she said. That always makes me mad. 'You're up early. Out of bed at eight o'clock on a Sunday morning? Things are looking up!'

I decided to kid her along a bit. I put on a scared, trembly voice. 'Listen, Beth — there's someone in the cupboard! Someone's been stabbed — the blood's coming under the door!'

'Ha, ha. Try it again next year, wise guy.'

I might have known I couldn't fool *her*.

I went back into my room and flopped down on my bed. I fished my Bible out from under the bed and flipped the pages over.

Some people think the Bible's not for kids. But I have a special book of daily readings that tells you what part to read and where to find it, and then tells you what it means. When you can understand what you're reading, the Bible's not boring at all.

But somehow, today, I didn't feel like it, and I

shut the book again. What had happened to me? I remembered praying during the night, and how far away God had seemed. It wasn't usually like that.

I didn't feel like going to church this morning, either. Maybe I was coming down ill with something. Instead of putting on my best grey trousers I shoved my legs into my jeans, pulled on a tee-shirt and went downstairs.

'I feel awful, Dad,' I said at breakfast. 'I've got a rotten stomach-ache and I feel sick. Can I stay at home this morning?'

'Two bowls of cornflakes and three slices of toast might have something to do with it.' He grinned and felt my forehead. 'I'll pray for you,' he said.

I should have known better than to ask — my dad can always tell if a stomach-ache's real or not.

It's not that I mind going to church, usually. It's OK. Our church isn't one of those places that's like a museum, all cold and empty and silent, where people say 'Shush!' if you talk too loud.

Before we started going there — which was at the beginning of last year — my dad used to shout at me and Beth all the time, and swear. Then, when we were in bed, you could hear him shouting at my mother, and she'd shout back, and the next day she'd be crying. It was awful.

It was a guy in the factory where my dad works who told him about this church, and one Sunday morning Dad made us get ready. He said we were all going there. Mum and Beth didn't seem to mind so much, but I didn't want to go. I thought I'd be bored out of my mind.

But when we got there, the people were singing a lively song, and clapping, and they all looked as if they were enjoying themselves. They even had a band at the front, playing drums and guitars and all that. It was great.

We had a good time that day, so after that we started going every week. Before long Mum and Dad were talking about Jesus, not in the way I'd always thought of him, as a God somewhere up in heaven minding his own business, but like he was a real person who mattered to them all of a sudden, and who really cared about what they did.

I didn't understand it all at the time. But it really made a difference, them being Christians. Nowadays they don't shout and swear at each other so much!

This Sunday, though, standing there and singing the songs with everybody else, I felt rotten. I couldn't join in like I usually do — I didn't want to pretend I was happy when I wasn't.

One of the songs we sang was 'Be bold, be strong,

for the Lord your God is with you...I am not afraid, I am not dismayed'.

My friend Andy, who was sitting next to me, turned round and grinned at me. But I couldn't smile back. It was a good song, but I was singing a lie. Because I *was* afraid.

'For the Lord your God is with you,' the song went on.

God was there, all the time, just like he always had been. So why couldn't I *feel* that he was with me?

It was OK during the day, when the sun was shining. But what about tonight, when the darkness came again?

What would my nightmare be tonight?

6

Light fingers

'Smokers' Corner', round by the third years' terrapin classroom, is a place I usually avoid. I don't smoke, and I don't aim to start, either. Smoking's a mug's game.

Sophie Batchelor calls the crowd that hangs out there the 'lung cancer club', so I was surprised to see her there with Zac and Robbo and some others. I hadn't been going to stop, but Zac turned round and saw me.

'Hi — Matt!' he shouted.

I strolled across, hoping they weren't going to start passing cigs around. What they do usually is, someone will light one up and then pass it around so that everybody can have a drag.

'Did you see the football match on telly yesterday?' Zac said. He was lying full length on the wall with his head on a pile of coats. 'Three-nil!

I ask you! They played like a bunch of ballet dancers at a picnic. That last goal was pitiful — I could have saved that with one arm tied behind me. I've never seen such rubbish.'

I dumped my bag on the ground and my anorak on the wall with the rest — it was a warm morning — and said, 'No. I didn't see it. My mum was watching a film. Looks like I didn't miss much.'

'You were lucky,' Robbo said. 'I wish *I'd* missed it.'

'Our television has a little button on the front,' said Sophie sarcastically. 'You push the button and the set goes off. You should try it sometime.'

'Talking of films, though,' Zac went on, 'there was a good late movie on last night — it didn't finish till after one o'clock. All blood and gore.'

'I saw that,' said Robbo, pinching out a cigarette end and tossing it under a bush. 'The Thing that grows inside this guy? He's OK till The Thing needs to get out. Then....'

'Yes, well,' Sophie broke in. 'Some of us need our beauty sleep. No wonder Zac nods off in Sweetie Pye's maths lessons if that's the time he usually goes to bed.'

'Not *usually,*' Zac told her. 'Only when there's a good film on. *Some* people,' he added, looking at me, 'are too chicken to watch such horrid, nasty things.'

What did he want to say that for? Had he told the others about that video we watched at his house on Saturday night? I hoped he wasn't going to turn out to be one of the sort that talk about their mates behind their backs.

Just then, the bell went for registration, and I wasn't sorry. After calling the register, Mrs Gray told us that the headmaster had arranged a special assembly, so we all trooped downstairs to the main hall. Mr Turner was looking grimmer than usual, so we knew it had to be something pretty bad.

He waited for silence, then stood glaring down at us. I wondered what was coming.

'I asked you all in here this morning to discuss with you a very serious matter.'

He *said* 'discuss', but we knew he'd be doing all the talking.

'On Friday morning, John Riley brought £5 to school with him — the idiot — to buy cassette recordings from another boy. During the lunch break that £5 disappeared.

'Someone in this school. . . .' He paused to let the words sink in. 'I repeat — someone — knows where that money went to. This is the most serious of a whole series of recent thefts. And incidents like this are happening far too often.

'Now, I do not intend to put up with this kind of thing in my school. I strongly advise the thief to come and see me — believe me, it's better to own up now than for me to have to bring the police into school. But bring them in I will, if I have not heard from the culprit by the end of the day.'

He had no chance. He must have known that.

He glared, scowling, around the room again. 'In the meantime, until the thief is caught, I advise you all very strongly to keep your money at home. Do not bring spare cash to school with you for any reason. That is all — you may return to your classes.'

The headmaster left the platform amid a sudden gabble of voices.

'I had fifty pence in my pencil case last week, and that went missing,' I heard a fat girl say, just in front of me. 'I thought I'd lost it, but now I'm not so sure. I had to go without chocolate that day.'

'Do you good, Fatso. Slim you off a bit,' a boy told her without sympathy.

'I wonder who the thief is,' Jacko Robinson said.

'Someone you wouldn't dream of suspecting,' Kelly Paget told him.

'Hey — I bet it's old Sweetie Pye!'

I didn't say anything, because I'd just had an uncomfortable thought. There was *one* light-fingered person in the school that I knew of.

Zac called it 'nicking' — he'd turned it into a game, and made it sound like he had the right to take money from his mum's purse — but it was stealing just as much as if he'd broken into a house and taken it from somebody he didn't know. What if it was him?

Should I say something? Go and tell Mr Turner? But how could I? After all, I didn't *know* it was Zac. It could just as easily have been somebody else. And anyway, Zac was my friend. Friends should stick together, shouldn't they?

Suddenly, I didn't know what was right and what was wrong. If it *was* him, I hoped God would let them find out without any help from me!

I found myself watching Zac all that morning. I had an idea that if he *was* the thief, he'd be looking guilty and worried.

I thought he'd feel like I had when I swiped a pack of chocolate biscuits from the pantry and scoffed the lot. I was only a little kid and I was terrified my mother would find out that it was me — I kept hoping, somehow, that she'd forget she'd bought them. Or that she'd blame it on Beth. I was sick with worry, and sick with chocolate, too!

She did find out, of course, and made me go without sweets for two whole weeks. I remember thinking that was a bit unfair. I'd reckoned that the being sick part had been enough punishment!

But although I kept an eye on Zac, I couldn't see that he felt anything like that. He was his usual clownish self. He livened up the biology lesson by mixing the results of a starch test we'd been doing. And in games he secretly climbed up and tied knots in the bottoms of the nets on the netball pitch. It couldn't have been him.

I looked for him at lunch-time but he was nowhere to be seen. And his seat was empty all afternoon. I wondered where he could be.

'Where's Zac?' Kelly Paget said to me when the bell went for the end of school. She's gone on Zac, in spite of the spider incident. But he thinks she's ugly. He calls her 'Horse-face' behind her back.

I shrugged my shoulders. 'He didn't tell me. Perhaps he's skiving. I didn't see him in the canteen at dinner-time.'

'I've never known him skive off school before. But why else would he go home? He wasn't ill, was he?' She sounded concerned. 'It's the form trip on Friday.'

Mr Newton had organised a history trip to some cathedral or other. I'd got my name down for it, and I knew Zac had. However deadly it turned out to be, it couldn't be worse than school. We've got double maths on Fridays.

'Zac was all right this morning,' I said. 'If he'd been ill he wouldn't have shinned up those netball posts and tied the nets up.'

She giggled in that stupid way some girls have. 'Did he do that?' she asked. 'I didn't see him. I don't know how he thinks up so many things to do. He put a dead frog in Sophie Batchelor's pocket yesterday. I've never known anybody like him.'

Neither had I, and neither had anybody else. I think that's why all the kids like and admire him. And why the teachers can't stand him!

I shoved my maths books into my bag — we'd had a peaceful maths lesson for a change, without Zac.

I was the last out of our room. It felt funny, walking home on my own.

I'd just decided to call round at his house to find out where he'd been all afternoon when I saw him, sitting on the wall by the chemist's shop with his hands stuck in his pockets. It looked like he was waiting for me. I crossed the road.

'Hi!' I said. 'I was just going round to your house. What's up? You look like a turkey on Christmas Eve!'

He stood up and faced me, smiling. It wasn't a pleasant smile. 'I might have known you'd pretend not to know anything about it,' he said.

'About what? Come on, Zac — I've got no idea what you're talking about.'

'Oh, very good! What marvellous acting!'

'Zac, I mean it. What am I supposed to have done?'

'It made you feel really good, didn't it?' he said. His eyes narrowed, making his face ugly and hard. 'Well, I hope you enjoyed yourself, because that's the last thing you'll enjoy for a long time. Believe me, I'm going to make you very sorry.'

'Zac? Zac!'

But he had turned away and was marching down the road. I stood there staring after him with my mouth open.

'Catching flies?'

It was Robbo, on his way to the Corner Cabin. There's always a crowd around the sweet shop after school.

'Zac's just gone mad,' I told him.

'Well, you can't blame him, can you? I'd be mad, too, if you'd grassed on *me* like that.'

'Grassed on him?' I was beginning to see light. 'He thinks I . . .? What's he been telling you?' I was getting mad, and I could feel my cheeks growing hot. 'I haven't done a single thing!'

Robbo shrugged. 'Zac thinks you have. He says

you told the headmaster he nicked Riley's money on Friday. Turner sent for him at dinner-time and kept him down there for ages, asking him questions about it.'

'And *was* it him?' I couldn't help asking.

'I dunno. He says not. But after that, Mr Turner sent him home to think it over, and told him to come back tomorrow with the truth.'

'But what made him think *I* told on him?'

'He says it couldn't have been anybody else. He didn't say much about that, but it's something about you going round to his house on Saturday night.'

I knew it. I'd seen him pinching money from his mother, and Zac had put two and two together and made half a dozen.

I said, 'He's crazy if he thinks I told Turner anything about that.'

'Well, if you did, you're a rotten sort of friend to have, that's all I can say.'

'Look, I didn't. Right?'

I might have *thought* about it, but I hadn't *done* it, had I? Obviously, I wasn't the only one in the school who knew what Zac was really like. Somebody else knew him at least as well as I did. Somebody who was prepared to go to Mr Turner about it. Who could it have been? I only knew that it wasn't me.

Zac was sure it was, though. And he'd said he'd make me sorry. As if I didn't already have enough to worry about! What was he planning?

I couldn't guess. I only knew that, whatever it was, I wasn't going to like it.

7

A set-up

You've heard that saying about your heart being in your boots? I'd never known what that really felt like before.

But the next morning when I was on my way to school I went warily around every street corner, wondering if Zac had got some other kids together to ambush me and beat me up. I haven't been in a fight for a long time, but I knew myself well enough to guess that I wouldn't stand much of a chance against more than one at a time.

But I got into the classroom without any trouble, and I was already sitting at my desk when Zac came in. I was astonished when he gave me a lop-sided grin and said, 'Hi!'

I couldn't understand it. The last thing he'd said was that he was going to make me sorry — he'd been ready to knock my teeth in. Now here he was, behaving as though nothing had happened. Why would he do that? What was he up to now?

But that wasn't being fair to him. I told myself that I ought to be glad. Perhaps he'd had second thoughts. He'd realised that, after all, I hadn't said anything to Mr Turner about him. Or he'd found out who really *had* grassed on him. Either way, it looked as if he'd decided to let bygones be bygones.

I hoped I was right — having enemies is uncomfortable. You never know when they'll try to get at you.

At the beginning of mid-morning break a third-former came in with a message that Zac was to go and see the headmaster.

We walked down the stairs together like we always did — the canteen is on the same side of the school as the headmaster's office — but I felt tongue-tied. What did he expect me to say to him? Should I ask what made him change his mind about me? Or should I just wish him good luck with Turner?

Then he dropped his bombshell.

Right out of the blue he said to me, 'You going to Batchelor's party on Sunday?'

He produced a paper bag and offered me a treacle toffee, just as if he couldn't care less that he was on his way to a rotten interview with the headmaster. I wondered if he'd pinched some money to buy the sweets.

I said, 'No thanks,' and he stuffed the bag back in his pocket.

'Yes, I'm going,' I told him. 'My mother says I have to.' I didn't want him to get the idea that I really *wanted* to go. 'Are you?'

'Yeah — course I am!'

He sounded eager. That wasn't like Zac. He has the same opinion of Sophie Batchelor as I do. I must have looked surprised, because he said, 'I wouldn't miss it for anything. I happen to know what they're planning.'

'What?' I didn't like the tone of his voice. It sounded as if they were planning something he knew I wouldn't like.

'They're hiring a video,' he told me with relish. 'The guy at the video shop promised to reserve it for them. It's fantastic — I've seen it before. It's even better than the one we saw at my house the other night. *Creeping Flesh!* We're going to have a great time!'

* * *

For the rest of that week I could think about nothing but that awful party. It seemed as if I spent the biggest part of every day dreaming up ways of getting out of going. I'd rather have been having all my teeth out at the dentist's. Or be sick with mumps like Chris Jennings.

Looking back, I don't know why it never occurred to me to tell my mother the truth. That way, I'd have got out of going to the party straightaway. She hates those films as much as my dad does — and now I know why.

There's a lot of things like that, when you come to think about it. Your parents tell you not to do something, but you do it anyway, just to see what it's like. Then you realise that they were right all along — but by that time you're in a mess!

Zac never did tell me what Mr Turner said to him. But after that he never stopped talking about *Creeping Flesh*. Twenty times over, I heard all the rotten details about it — who got killed by the zombies, how much they screamed when they were being tortured and exactly how they died. He knew jolly well that I didn't want to go and see it.

He was putting on an act with me, pretending to be my friend. Even when we were queueing for the coach for the school trip he stood with me, as if we were going to sit together as usual.

We were just going to get on the coach when this kid I didn't know came up and said that Mr Pye wanted to see me. I told Zac to save me a seat and nipped back into school.

I knew I'd have to be quick, as the coach left at 9.30, and it was 20 past already. So I charged down the corridor, looking in every classroom, and was shouted at by Mrs Gray for running in school.

After hunting all over the place, I eventually ran old Sweetie to earth in the staffroom.

He looked at me suspiciously, as if I was trying to be funny, then told me he'd never sent for me at all.

It was twenty to ten when I got back to the coach, and everybody was inside it but me. Mr Newton was pacing up and down, looking at his watch, waiting for me to turn up.

He started shouting at me straightaway, so I hopped on the bus sharpish, with rows of grinning faces watching me. Obviously they were all in on the joke. I walked forward — and stopped dead.

The only empty seat on the coach was next to Sophie Batchelor. Zac was sitting across the gangway with Kelly Paget. I tapped her on the shoulder. 'Change places!' I hissed.

I should have saved my breath, because Kelly obviously thought Zac was the best thing since sliced bread. And she wasn't going to let go of him in a hurry. Sitting next to her wasn't troubling Zac too much either, I noticed. I don't suppose she'd any idea how often he'd called her 'Horse-face' when she wasn't around. I felt like telling her.

Zac had gone to an awful lot of trouble to arrange all this.

'Matt Graham — with your co-operation we could tell the driver that we are at last ready to move off. Or perhaps you are intending to stand up all the way to Hernwell?'

My face must have been as red as a tomato. I sat down, leaving as much space between me and Sophie as I could without falling off the edge of the seat.

Robbo was sitting in front of Zac, and he turned around and grinned, first at him, then at me.

'Don't you dare say anything!' I told him.

All he said was, 'Have a nice day!' and winked at me.

'Great,' I thought.

Some nice day I was going to have, poking around old cathedrals and stuff.

Not to mention being tied to Sophie Batchelor for the whole trip!

'Just us'

Sophie said nothing at all. She just kept staring out of the window so I couldn't see anything of her face. I noticed, though, that the tip of her right ear was very pink. I wondered if she was hating this as much as I was!

Zac and Robbo started talking. Kelly looked a bit peeved. She'd thought she had Zac to herself.

'Have you seen *Creeping Flesh?*' Zac asked him, loud enough for me to hear.

'No. What's it about?'

'It starts with this nuclear war that wipes out most of the population. That part's good — you see people's faces melting away in the heat. Wait till you see it! But the best bit's when the melted-away ones come to life again as zombies, with all the flesh hanging off them. Man — you should see them — and they live off the few normal ones left.

'You've never seen anything like this film. Batchelor's dad's reserved it for the party — hasn't he, Sophie?'

Sophie nodded, but she didn't say anything.

I tried hard not to listen, but they were talking so loud you couldn't miss a thing. Half the bus could hear them.

To my relief, once we'd left the town behind us and got properly going, Mr Newton stood up at the front of the coach and clapped his hands for silence. A lot of the teachers do that and nobody takes any notice. Some of the kids even clap back at them. You couldn't do that with Old Newton.

It took a minute or two to shut Zac and Robbo up, but before long he could make himself heard.

He had a sheaf of papers in his hands. 'I am going to give each of you one of these,' he said, 'and I expect you all to work hard at filling them in throughout the day. Part one contains questions on Hernwell Cathedral, which we shall visit this morning. This afternoon we move on to the Manor House, and you will find that the questions in part two relate to that.'

He passed our seat and gave a paper to me and one to Sophie. I looked at it. Number one on the sheet had a drawing of an ugly face, with ears like a bat and a pair of horns on its head. It said: 'Write down the exact position of this gargoyle in the cathedral.'

I was still mad, so I got my pencil out and wrote 'Donald Cusack's face'.

Mr Newton must have seen me because he said, 'Keep these papers neat and tidy, and answer all the questions. The results, good or bad, will figure in your term's report.'

I wet the tip of a finger and rubbed at what I'd written but only made dirty marks and a hole in the paper. Sophie fished in her bag and passed me a rubber.

Then she held out a tube of sweets. 'Have one,' she said.

They were those fizzy Love Hearts — sweets with little messages written on them. The one I took said 'Fooled again'. I grinned and tossed it into my mouth.

I was glad when we got to Hernwell and the coach pulled up outside the cathedral. We all climbed out. It felt good to stretch my legs after all that sitting down.

A guy in a long black robe, who, we were told, was called a verger, took us all around the place, pointing out what he thought were the interesting bits. He was a good sort. He kept cracking jokes all the time, and that made the whole thing more bearable.

We looked at box pews and carved screens, flying buttresses and a chained-up Bible, writing down some of the answers to the questions on the sheets we'd been given.

The bones in the crypt were the best. The verger told us they were very ancient and had been dug up when they'd had some renovations done in the church.

After that we all went outside. The gargoyle in the picture was on a corner of the roof. Sophie nudged me and said, 'It *is* like Zac, isn't it?'

We both laughed and I felt a bit better. It made me feel that somebody was on my side, even if it was only Sophie Batchelor! I got the idea, somehow, that although this video was going to be at Sophie's party, she wasn't as keen on it as Zac and Robbo.

There was half an hour left before lunch and Mr Newton told us to wander around quietly, finishing off our question sheets. He and the verger went off to get a coffee somewhere.

It was a mistake to leave Zac to himself in a place like that.

First, he gathered up all the prayer-books and hid them under the little winding stairs that led up to the belfry. I bet they're still looking for them.

Then he got hold of a spare question sheet and

wrote on the back, 'Do not disturb — poker game in progress'. He stuck it on the vestry door with chewing gum instead of Blu-Tack.

He was just about to start experimenting with the bell-ropes when Mr Newton came back.

We all piled back into the coach and went off to have a picnic by the river. That was the best part of the day. The ducks were a scream, scooting about for bits of bread people threw for them.

Before long they were all up on the bank, milling round us like football hooligans. Lunging for crumbs, snatching them from each other, chasing up and down the bank trying to get more than the others. They had us in stitches.

The afternoon was much the same as the morning, only instead of looking at gargoyles and stuff, we looked at four-poster beds, a secret door and a bloodstain on the stone floor from when the lady of the house threw herself off the balcony. (Sophie says they freshen the stain up with red paint every year or two, but I don't know whether that's true.)

This lady is supposed to walk there as a ghost. I asked the man who was showing us round if he'd seen her, but he hadn't.

Zac wasn't talking so much about his rotten film on the way home. He found something else to do.

We were driving along this quiet country road when suddenly Kelly Paget let out this awful screech, like someone's burglar alarm going off.

'Get it off me! Get it *off!* Take it away, Zac!' And she started dancing around in the aisle. 'Where's it gone? Where *is* it?'

'What's up?' Sophie asked her.

'It's a frog!' Kelly's voice was squeaky with panic, and she looked three shades paler. 'He put a frog on my knee. I can't stand frogs.'

'Why not?' said Sophie. 'Frogs are all right.'

'Eeugh! How could you?'

Zac fished the frog out from under the seat. 'Here it is,' he said. He shoved it at Kelly's face and the siren set off again.

Mr Newton, at the front of the coach, clapped his hands. 'Less noise back there,' he shouted. But nobody took any notice of him.

Kelly went off up the bus and squeezed three on a seat with two other girls. Zac sat down again and started tormenting the frog.

First, he held it by one leg and watched it squirm and wriggle. Then he held it up in the air and let it jump off his hand so it had a long way to drop.

'Stop it!' shouted Sophie suddenly. 'Stop it this minute! How would you like someone to do that to *you?*'

He turned and grinned at her, twirling the frog around by one leg.

And suddenly, I saw red. At that moment I felt like I hated him.

I stood up, grabbed the frog off him before he knew what was happening, and ran down the bus with it. I asked the driver to stop so I could let it go, and he was so surprised that he did.

'Did we hurt the poor ickle froggie, den?' said Zac. He and Robbo were sitting together now.

I acted like he wasn't there. I sat down again in my seat and grinned at Sophie.

She smiled at me and after a minute passed me another sweet. This one said, 'Just us'. I felt my face start to go red.

I didn't eat the sweet. I put it in my pocket instead.

9

No way out

'Hey, Robbo,' Zac said loudly as we were getting off the coach at the end of the day. 'Why did the chicken run across the road?'

'I don't know,' Robbo said theatrically. 'Why did the chicken run across the road?'

'Because it didn't want to see the nasty video!'

They both fell about laughing. I wanted to push their faces in. Christians aren't supposed to feel like that about people, but I didn't care much just then.

Sophie gave me a funny look, like she wasn't sure what was going on, then took a breath to say something to Zac.

He cut her off. 'Right, Batchelor,' he said. 'We'll be round at your place on Sunday night.' He rubbed his hands together. 'I can't wait!'

Sophie waved a hand towards the school building. 'There's one down the corridor if you can't wait,' she said, and walked off.

'That's an old one,' he shouted after her. Then he turned to me. 'Only two more days now,' he said gleefully. 'You *are* going, aren't you?'

'Of course I am!' I told him.

How I wished I wasn't!

*   *   *

I didn't want Sunday to come, but it came anyway. You know how it is. At 7.25 on Sunday night I was standing in front of my bedroom mirror glumly running a comb through my hair. I was supposed to be getting ready for the party, but I was taking as long about it as I could.

Mum shouted up the stairs, 'Come on, Matt — hurry up! The card said the party started at 7.30, and it's nearly that now.'

I shut my eyes. 'Make them cancel the party,' I prayed desperately, without any real hope that it would happen. 'Or let Gran come so that I won't have to go to it.' Another idea struck me. 'Or let me get mumps like Chris Jennings. I don't care how much it hurts.'

My dad would have had a million fits if he'd heard that. In our house we don't pray to get sick. We pray about *not* getting stuff like mumps and chicken-pox. But how else was I to get out of it?

I swallowed, hard. Now I thought about it, my

throat *did* feel a bit sore. Did mumps start off with a sore throat? Gingerly, I prodded the sides of my neck with the tips of my fingers. They were swollen — I was sure they were.

I went downstairs very slowly.

'There you are at last,' my mother said. 'Now, don't go without the birthday card. You signed it, didn't you?'

'I don't feel so good, Mum. I don't think I ought to go.'

'You look fine. You'll see — once you get there, Matt, you'll have a fantastic time.'

'But I've got this sore throat. And I'm sure my neck's a bit swollen. I think I'm getting mumps. Chris Jennings has mumps and I sat next to him in assembly last week.'

She shoved Sophie's present at me. She'd wrapped it up in fancy paper and tied a red ribbon round it. 'Rubbish. You're as fit as a fiddle,' she said.

'Well, don't blame me if everybody at the party catches mumps off me.'

'I won't.'

I told myself that she didn't care. I could infect the whole town with mumps or bubonic plague or anything. What did it matter to her?

'And what if Gran comes?' I went on. She comes

over a lot on Sunday evenings. 'I wouldn't want
to miss her.'

'She's staying at Aunt Barbara's this weekend.
Remember?'

It seemed there was no way out of it.

I came out with the straight truth at last. 'Mum,
I don't want to go.'

But that just made her mad. 'Matthew!' (She
only calls me that when I've gone too far.) 'What
a fuss you're making — about nothing! All because
it's a girl's party. You can't just *not go* — not now,
when Mrs Batchelor's expecting you. We accepted
the invitation, remember? *And* bought Sophie a
present and a card. So you're going, and that's
that!'

'Mum....' I started to say something else, but
she wasn't listening.

'Have a good time, Matt. Tell Mrs Batchelor
there's no hurry to return the cake tin.'

I went out of the door and trailed slowly along
the street.

Have a good time! Huh! My mother thought she
was doing me such a big favour, sending me to that
party. I thought, 'If she only knew what she was
sending me to!'

But she didn't know because I hadn't told her.

And suddenly I knew that I wasn't being fair.

I'd been blaming her for the way I felt, when it was nothing to do with her.

I'd been blaming God, too, because he seemed so far away and hadn't been there when I needed him. But wasn't this whole thing my own stupid fault?

I'd known, right at the very beginning, that I shouldn't have been watching that film with Zac. But instead of saying so, and telling him I didn't want to see it, I'd followed him like a silly sheep. No wonder I couldn't find God. No wonder they called me chicken!

Zac's idea of a chicken was someone who was scared to watch those awful films. But I reckoned that a *real* chicken is someone who was scared to tell him what they thought of him and his rotten old *Creeping Flesh*.

The worst of it was that, if I was right, I was just as chicken as they said. Because I couldn't see myself having the guts to tell him just what I thought.

I remembered all the things Zac had said on the school trip about that video, and my own flesh crept at the thought of it. But it wouldn't only be Zac who would laugh at me.

How could I face a whole *roomful* of people — including Sophie Batchelor — making jokes about chickens?

10

Creeping flesh

I was the last to arrive at Sophie's. As I walked through the door I could hear a lot of talking and laughing. But it stopped suddenly when I went into the room, and they all looked guilty, like they'd been talking about me. You can always tell. I wondered what they'd been saying.

I said, 'What's up?'

Sophie replied, 'What do you mean? Nothing's up,' and Kelly Paget giggled and nearly choked. Apart from Sophie she was the only girl there. The rest were all boys from school, so things weren't so bad from that point of view.

Sophie put some noisy music on and she and Kelly prodded some of the guys and made them dance. Robbo didn't seem to mind. He thought he was good.

I called out, 'You should see yourself, Robbo —

you look like a grasshopper.'

'I don't see *you* doing any dancing. I bet you dance like a frog on a bed of nails.'

Kelly clapped her hands over her ears. 'Shut up about frogs!' she said. 'Don't remind me.'

'What did I say? Only that Matt's not dancing.'

Too right, I thought. Nobody's making *me* dance! They tried, though.

Sophie changed the record. 'We can do the Slosh to this one,' she said. 'Come on, Matt — join in.'

'No fear. I can't dance!'

'But the Slosh is easy. Come on, I'll show you.'

I shook my head. 'I'll sit here and watch.'

'Look,' Kelly said. 'One, two, three, kick, back, two, three, kick. . . .'

I watched.

'Come on. Now you try. Robbo couldn't do it before, could you, Rob?'

I shook my head. 'You must be joking! It's OK till you get to that ''clap, knees up, twiddle round'' bit. I'd never twiddle round in the right place.'

Sophie and Kelly looked at each other. Sophie winked. They both pounced on me and grabbed an arm each. I slid off the chair and landed in a heap on the floor. I stayed put.

'Zac — come and help! Pull him up. Make him dance.'

In the middle of all this, Sophie's poodle came running in, barking its head off as usual. I never was so glad to see a dog! Robbo was jigging away like a kangaroo and didn't see it.

'Watch out, Robbo — don't tread on my dog!' Sophie shouted.

'That's a *dog?*' he said, acting surprised. 'I've seen better-looking dishmops.'

'It might look OK if it was stuffed,' said Derek Briggs. 'Stuffed and mounted in a glass case!'

'She could stick its head on the wall like a hunting trophy,' suggested Zac, 'with an inscription on it: "The Woolly Wombat from Wigan — the last of its species."'

'You're trying too hard,' Sophie told him pityingly. 'Wombats come from Australia.' She took hold of the dog's collar. 'Come on, Lulu — come away from the nasty boys.'

'Lulu!' said Derek. 'I don't believe it. You don't call a dog *Lulu!*'

'It figures,' Zac said. 'That's not really a dog. Batchelor just *thinks* it is. Lulu — loo-brush. See the connection?' He held out his hand. 'Here, Loo-Brush. Come on, then.'

That daft dog trotted right up to him. 'See that? I told you. It knows its name. . . .'

Sophie went for Zac, bashing him over the head

with a rolled-up *TV Times,* and he was laughing fit to burst. 'Gerroff! Get her off me, somebody!' he yelled.

I pitied him. Sophie Batchelor could out-bash Stallone.

Things were just hotting up when Sophie's mother called out that supper was ready. There was a stampede.

I'd been wrong about the hot dogs — this time Mrs Batchelor had really gone to town. She'd sent out for Kentucky Fried Chicken and mountains of chips, and she'd made a blue and white cake in the shape of a launching pad, with a spaceship ready for take-off.

It all looked fantastic, but I knew, the minute I smelled the spicy-chicken smell, that I wouldn't be able to eat any of it. I hadn't had a thing to eat since lunchtime, but my stomach felt over-full just the same, as if I'd already eaten a four-course dinner. I felt queasy at the very thought of sitting down to chicken and chips.

Zac noticed that I wasn't eating anything — he would! — and he nudged Robbo and grinned.

When there were only piles of chicken bones and a quarter of the cake left, and nobody could eat another thing, we all trooped back into the lounge.

Zac rubbed his hands together as if he could

hardly wait. He was always doing that and I couldn't stand it.

'Now for the moment we've all been waiting for,' he said. Sophie switched on the TV and slotted a tape into the video.

'*Creeping Flesh*,' Zac said gleefully.

I slipped behind all the others, meaning to sit at the back where nobody could see me, but Zac held me by the arm and pulled me on to the sofa to sit with him.

'Me and Matt, we like this sort of stuff, don't we? We're going to grab a good seat, where we can see everything.'

Kelly giggled again and Sophie poked her in the ribs. 'Shut up. The film's starting.'

I felt sick inside. *Really* sick. My stomach suddenly churned as if I'd eaten that whole pile of chicken and chips by myself. I didn't want to watch this film — and everybody knew it. I felt as though every eye in the room was fixed on me. Watching to see what I would do. Waiting to call me chicken and have a good laugh.

What would Sophie think of me if I couldn't sit through a film? I fingered the sweet she'd given me. I still had it in my pocket.

Then, suddenly, I knew that it didn't matter at all what she or any of them thought.

'Help me, God.'

I said the words inside my head. I knew this time that he was listening — and this time I was believing that he was going to answer me.

My heart was thumping like a pile-driver. But what did I need to be scared for?

I was a Christian. And that meant I had Jesus inside me. It was watching all that junk that had filled me full of fear and made it seem like he'd gone away. It kind of cuts you off. But really, he'd been there all the time.

Suddenly, I knew that I was free and I was strong. I didn't have to be afraid any more. What really mattered was doing what was right — and that would take *real* guts. I wasn't chicken at all!

I took a deep breath. 'Does everybody *really* want to watch this garbage?' I said. My voice was strong and steady. 'I know I'd rather be kicking a ball around in the park.'

'We know you would, too!' Derek clucked like a chicken — and I found I didn't care.

'Saint Matthew wants to go home,' said Zac. 'He thinks it's sinful to watch such evil films.'

'Yes, I do,' I said. 'And so would you if you had any sense.' I stood up. 'Anybody coming with me?'

'Sit down, Matt,' roared Derek from behind. 'I can't see!'

Somebody started to laugh, and Robbo poked me in the ribs. 'Look at that!' he said.

I glanced round at the TV set. The film title was just coming up on the screen.

It was *The Cat from Outer Space*.

11

Sophie's secret

A Disney film! I couldn't believe it.

'Look at his face. Just look at him!'

Sophie pressed the 'stop' button, laughing like crazy. Zac and Robbo were falling about, holding on to each other.

'He took it all in. He believed every word I told him!' Zac gasped, wiping his eyes. '*Creeping Flesh!* Oh, my God — I thought I'd *split,* trying not to laugh!'

I could feel my face turning bright red. Zac had set all this up. This was what he meant when he said I'd be sorry. He'd planned to make me look a fool in front of everybody.

A fine friend he'd turned out to be! There were a million rotten things I could have said to him, but I didn't say them. What I *did* say was, 'Don't talk about God that way,' and they all laughed again.

'I thought you were going to give the game away, Kelly, giggling like that!'

'Well, I couldn't help it.'

'You guys should have been there the other night when we were watching *Ghouls from the Pit of Hell,*' said Zac. 'It was worth a tenner of anybody's money to see him! Holding his breath. Closing his eyes so he couldn't see the nasty bits. God! His face was *green!*'

I looked at Zac as if I'd never seen him before. Sitting there, his head thrown back, hair all anyhow, and face twisted into an ugly laugh. I could see all the fillings in his back teeth.

He wasn't my friend. He never had been. A *real* friend cared about not hurting your feelings, but Zac was the sort of kid who just used people, even if it was only to get a good laugh.

In a funny way, I realised that I'd known from the very beginning what he was really like. My mum had been right about him — only I hadn't wanted to admit it, even to myself. What had I seen in him? I couldn't even remember.

'I'm going home,' I said.

'Don't hurry back,' Robbo shouted.

'Aw, come *on,* Matt!' said Zac. 'Aren't you staying to watch the film?' And they all laughed again.

Zac wiped his eyes and pushed his hanky back into his pocket. 'That's the best laugh I've had since Frank was in the loft and put his foot through the bedroom ceiling,' he said.

'I'm glad you enjoyed yourself,' I said, coldly.

'I really made you squirm, didn't I?' he went on. 'You were as sick as a cat, worrying about *Creeping Flesh* all week...just like I wanted you to! I told you you'd be sorry. You won't grass on me again in a hurry.'

Sophie glanced round. 'What do you mean?'

'I mean, nobody grasses on me and gets away with it.'

I said, 'I told you before, Zac. I don't know who told Turner you nicked Riley's fiver. I only know it wasn't me.'

'Tell me another.'

'That's the truth.'

'Hey — hang on a minute.' Sophie's cheeks had gone pink. 'You're saying *Matt* got you into trouble with the headmaster?'

'Of course he did. Who else would it be?'

Sophie stood up. Her eyes blazed and her cheeks were scarlet. 'It was me!' She shouted the words. 'I told Mr Turner you were the thief.'

'I don't believe you.'

'Believe what you want.'

'Right. I will. I know very well it wasn't you. Do you think we don't all know you're gone on Matt? Of course you'd say anything to cover up for him.'

'I'm not staying here to listen to this,' I said and headed for the door. 'See you around.'

Sophie shouted after me, 'Matt — don't go. Matt...I want to tell you something!'

But I went out and slammed the door after me.

It was true that Sophie liked me. You don't give Love Hearts with 'Just us' to someone you can't stand the sight of. But how come they all knew about it? I squirmed inside.

And telling lies to cover up for me! She needn't bother, I told myself grimly. That *couldn't* be true, or she wouldn't have helped them pull that video stunt. I threw the Love Heart into the gutter and ground it in with my heel.

'Matt!' Sophie was following me. I was nearly home. I turned into our gateway.

'Matt — wait. I've got something to tell you.'

'OK. So tell me.' It had better be good, I thought, after what happened back there.

But she just stood there, looking at me.

'This video thing — it wasn't my idea, Matt,' she said at last.

'You don't have to tell me that,' I said. 'I know

very well whose idea it was. But you went along
with it just the same, didn't you?'

'It was just a joke.'

'Well, I'm glad you found it funny.'

'I didn't know then why Zac was doing it. He
told me it was a practical joke. We all thought it
was funny — until he started poking fun at you
about watching that film with him the other night,
and making out you were chicken and all that. Then
I was sorry. It wasn't funny anymore. It was a
rotten thing to do.'

She put her hand on my arm and I let it stay
there. I only hoped that Beth wasn't looking out
of her bedroom window — I'd never hear the last
of it if she saw that.

'I once saw one of those films myself.' Sophie
whispered it like she was confessing to murder. She
tightened her grip and I could feel her nails digging
into my arm, even through my sleeve.

'It was last summer, when I was staying with my
Aunt Linda in Cornwall. My cousin Tim borrowed
this film from a friend of his, and hid it behind the
books in his bookcase until my aunt and uncle went
out. Tim dared me to watch it with him, with all
the lights out.'

I could imagine it. Sophie would have *had* to
watch it just to prove she was as good as any boy.

'Yeah? What was it like?'

She shuddered. 'I had nightmares about it for weeks after. Even now, I can't bear to think about it. So I know what you feel like — and laughing about it's a lousy trick. I wanted you to know. I never told anybody before — and I'll *kill* you if you ever breathe a word to a single soul!' She took her hand away.

I said, 'I won't tell.'

She sighed. 'When it was too late, I wished I'd never watched the rotten thing, but I'd never have lived it down if I hadn't. It seemed like a brave thing to do at the time.'

'Yeah.'

It was comforting, somehow, to know that somebody else felt the way I did. Even if it was only Sophie Batchelor — and she's a girl!

You know that boys are supposed to be tough, so you'll do anything rather than have people laugh at you and think you're wet. And if you're a Christian as well, it seems worse than ever because that gives them something else to laugh at you for.

'Zac ruined my party,' Sophie went on. 'I should never have asked him. But I thought that if I didn't invite him he'd smell a rat — and I didn't want him to know I was the one who told Mr Turner about him.'

'So it's true? It really *was* you?'

She nodded, slowly. 'All week he's been thinking it was *you,* and I didn't know. And he was planning all along to use my party to get even with you! He's a louse.'

'But what made you go to Mr Turner? You couldn't possibly have known that Zac took Riley's money. Nobody knows for sure, even now, whether he did or not. He's not saying.'

Sophie sat down on our garden wall and started picking at a piece of loose mortar. I was glad my dad couldn't see her.

'I didn't mention John Riley or his money to Mr Turner. I just told him about the money he stole from *me.*'

I looked up sharply. 'Zac took money from you? When?'

She sighed. 'It was that same day. You remember? We were all talking in Smoker's Corner. Zac was lying on the wall....'

'I remember. He was talking about his rotten films even then.'

'There was a pound coin in my anorak pocket,' Sophie said. 'I'd been going to have a school dinner and I had to go home for lunch instead. I knew the money was there — I'd had it in my hand just the minute before. But when the bell went I felt for it and it had gone.'

'And Zac was the only one who went near the coats,' I broke in. 'He had his head on them! It had to be him. Why didn't you accuse him there and then?'

She shrugged. 'Too chicken, I expect.' She slid me a glance out of the corner of her eye and grinned.

I grinned back.

It was good to be able to smile again. It felt as if a load had gone from my mind!

'It took a lot of guts to come out with what you said to them back there,' Sophie went on. 'And Zac knew it, too. He tries to make out you're chicken but I was watching his face. His big scheme to make you look silly fell as flat as a flounder!'

She gave me a sideways glance. 'Your religion means a lot to you, doesn't it?' she said. 'I mean, it really seems to work.'

'It's not religion,' I told her. 'It's having Jesus in your life.' And I knew that before today I'd never have had the courage to say that to anybody.

Sophie pulled a face. But I guessed that from now on she'd listen to what I said about being a Christian, because she'd seen what God could do. And if he'd taken *my* fear away, he could do it for *her,* too!

After all, who cares what those wallies say about me? I'd rather be called a chicken any day than have a mind full of garbage.

Because I know that *God is on my side* — and so is Sophie Batchelor!